The United Kingdom

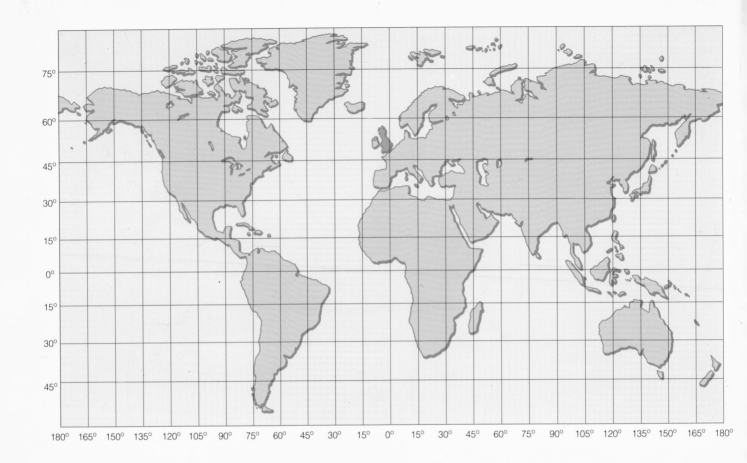

ATLANTIC

OCEAN

ORKNEY
ISLANDS

SHETLAND
ISLANDS

THE
UNITED
KINGDOM

N

W E

S

OUTER HEBRIDES

INNER HEBRIDES

SCOTLAND

Aberdeen

NORTH

SEA

Glasgow
Edinburgh

55°

Londonderry

N. IRELAND
Belfast

Newcastle upon Tyne

Middlesbrough

IRISH
SEA

York

Preston   Leeds

Liverpool   Manchester

IRELAND

Nottingham

ENGLAND

Birmingham

WALES

LONDON

Swansea
Cardiff

Bristol

Southampton

Plymouth

ENGLISH CHANNEL

0°

0   100 mi

250 km

FRANCE

The United Kingdom

David Flint

RAINTREE STECK-VAUGHN
PUBLISHERS

Austin, Texas

Design	Roger Kohn
Editors	Penny Clarke, Helene Resky
DTP editor	Helen Swansbourne
Picture research	Valerie Mulcahy
Illustration	János Márffy
	Coral Mula
Consultant	Robert G. Ford, University of Birmingham
Commissioning editor	Debbie Fox

We are grateful to the following for permission
to reproduce photographs:
Front Cover: Robert Harding Picture Library *above*, Tony Stone
Worldwide *below;* Allsport, page 22 *above* (Steve Morton);
Keith Cardwell/TRIP, page 19; J. Allan Cash, page 30;
Central Office of Information, page 24; Eastbourne Tourism
& Leisure, page 17; Energy Technology Support Unit, page 42;
The Environmental Picture Library, page 39 (A. Greig); Eye
Ubiquitous/TRIP, pages 8 and 31 (Chris Bland), 23 (Davey
Bold); Sally & Richard Greenhill, page 18; Robert Harding
Picture Library, page 22 *below;* The Image Bank, pages 33
(Jeff Smith), 36 (John Hill); Levy McCallum Advertising, page
41; Life File/TRIP, page 29 (Lee Nixon); Magnum, page 37 (Ian
Berry); Metropolitan Police, page 25; Network, page 20 *above*
(Matthews); Picturepoint, pages 16, 20 *below*, 32 *left* and *right*,
34; Q. A. Photos Ltd., page 9; Rex Features, pages 13 *above
left*, 13 *below*, 40; Tony Stone Worldwide, pages 10 (David H.
Endershee), 13 *above right*, 15 *above* and *below*, 27 (Trevor
Wood), 29 (Phil Matt), 38/39 (Colin Prior); The Telegraph
Colour Library, pages 14, 26; Zefa, pages 11, 21.

The statistics given in this book are the most up to date
available at the time of going to press

Printed and bound in Hong Kong by
Paramount Printing Group Ltd

1 2 3 4 5 6 7 8 9 0 HK 99 98 97 96 95 94

Library of Congress Cataloging-in-Publication Data

Flint, David. 1946–
The United Kingdom / David Flint.
p. cm. – (Country fact files)
Includes index.
Summary: Discusses the geography, population, daily life,
industries, environment, and future of Great Britain.
ISBN 0-8114-1849-9
1. Great Britain – Juvenile literature. [1. Great Britain.]
I. Title. II. Series. DA27.5.F57 1994
941–dc20
93–13610
CIP AC

CONTENTS

Words that are explained in the glossary are printed in
SMALL CAPITALS the first time they are mentioned in the text.

⚜ INTRODUCTION

The United Kingdom (or Great Britain) is made up of England, Wales, Scotland, and Northern Ireland. The country has changed greatly in the last 20 years and is continuing to change. Some of the major changes include the following:

● Some farmland in the countryside is no longer being used to grow crops or graze animals. This unused land is being put to other uses, for example, theme parks or riding stables.

● Towns continue to grow and expand into surrounding areas of the countryside.

● Town centers are being knocked down and redeveloped.

● More people are leaving cities to live in villages in the countryside where they commute to work.

● Old industries, like steel and shipbuilding, are declining and are being replaced by new ones, such as electronics and computer manufacturing

● New highways are being built to relieve congestion on the roads, but, as a result, valuable countryside is often lost.

● New sources of energy that do not pollute the ENVIRONMENT, such as wind and wave power, are being developed.

● People are becoming more aware of the need to look after the environment, and the number of projects to recycle glass, textiles, and paper is increasing.

● Large, out-of-town shopping centers are

becoming increasingly popular, but they take customers away from traditional city-based shops and rely on people reaching them by car.
● In general, people are living longer thanks to medical advances. However, this means many more facilities for the elderly will be needed in the future.

As the United Kingdom changes, it adapts to changes in the rest of the world. The U.K. depends on the rest of the world for imports of a wide range of goods, from timber, coal, and iron ore to cars, computers, and television sets. The U.K. also depends on selling its exports to the rest of the world, especially its oil, its manufactured goods, such as cars, and its services, such as banking and insurance.

◀ New developments, like the Canary Wharf project in London's Docklands, aim to improve run-down areas.

▲ The Channel Tunnel marks an important new link between the U.K. and the rest of Europe.

THE UNITED KINGDOM AT A GLANCE

● Area

U.K.	94,217 square miles	(244,100 sq. km.)
England	50,331 square miles	(130,439 sq. km.)
Scotland	30,410 square miles	(78,772 sq. km.)
Wales	8,016 square miles	(20,768 sq. km.)
N. Ireland	5,462 square miles	(14,121 sq. km.)

● Population (1991)

U.K.	57.4 million
England	47.8 million
Scotland	5.1 million
Wales	2.9 million
N. Ireland	1.6 million

● Population density: 588 per square mile (235 per sq. km.) (U.K.)
● Capital: London, population 6.7 million
● Other main cities: Birmingham 1 million
    Glasgow 734,000
    Leeds 712,000
    Sheffield 526,000
    Liverpool 463,000
    Manchester 449,000
    Edinburgh 439,000
    Bristol 391,000
    Cardiff 388,000
    Belfast 374,000
    Newcastle upon Tyne 278,000
    Swansea 168,000
 ● Longest river: Thames, 279 miles (450 km)
 ● Highest mountain: Ben Nevis, 4,413 feet (1,344 m)
 ● Language: English
 ● Main religion: Christianity
 ● Currency: Pound sterling, written as £
 ● Economy: Highly industrialized
● Major resources: Coal, oil, natural gas
● Major products: Automobiles, machinery, chemicals
● Environmental problems: Some pollution of rivers and coasts, especially around the North Sea and the Irish Sea.

THE LANDSCAPE

The United Kingdom has a very varied landscape — from mountains to moorlands, and deep valleys to steep cliffs. In general, the older rocks, like granite and basalt, are igneous rocks. They were formed from hot molten material that flowed out from beneath the earth's crust. Igneous rocks are more resistant to erosion and stand out as highland areas. These highland areas are mostly in the northern and western regions, like Wales, the Lake District, and Scotland. Ice has worn away the land to create deep U-shaped valleys and long lakes. Because these upland areas usually have thin acid soils, they are covered by heather, moss, or poor grassland. Only in the valleys that cut into the uplands is farming profitable.

In the south and east the younger, softer rocks have weathered creating a fertile soil and some of the country's best farmland. These areas are mainly composed of

Spey River
Dee River
Ben Nevis 4,413 ft (1,344 m)
Tweed River
Bann River
LAKE DISTRICT
Tees River
Ouse River
Mersey River
Snowdon 3,562 ft (1,085 m)
Trent River
Severn River
Thames River
Exe River

0   100 mi
250 km

N

◀ **The Lake District is a glaciated highland area.**

▲ **The west and north are higher than the south or east.**

sedimentary rock, like sandstone, which was formed when sand, mud, fine gravel or other eroded material were compressed into rocks. The higher ground of the chalk hills of the Cotswolds or Chilterns interrupt these farmland areas.

A third type of rock, metamorphic rock, is found in areas, such as southern Scotland and the coast of Northern Ireland. Slate and other metamorphic rocks were originally igneous or sedimentary rocks but were later changed by heat and pressure.

◀ *The Thames Barrier is an important defense against the flooding of London. When sea levels rise the gates are raised. Since its opening in 1987, the Thames Barrier gates have, so far, not been needed.*

As the ice locked up in the ice caps of the North and South Poles melts, sea level rises. This rise in sea level has drowned valleys in Devon and Cornwall to create inlets called RIAS. In Scotland, the rising sea level has created SEA-LOCHS and FJORDS.

U.K. LAND USE (1991)
(percent)

- Other (e.g., bare rock) 6.7
- Towns, cities, roads, and factories 8.4
- Woodland 8.7
- Arable (crops) 29.0
- Permanent pasture grass 21.3
- Rough grazing (rough grass and moorland) 25.9

KEY FACTS

● Nowhere in the U.K. is more than 62 miles (100 km) from the sea.

● Cliffs south of Bridlington on the east coast of England are being eroded by the sea at the rate of 7 feet (2 m) a year.

● The sea level around the U.K. has risen by about 3 feet (1 m) since 1900 and is still rising.

● Limestone rocks are quarried for use in making cement, aspirin, paper, and chocolate!

CLIMATE AND WEATHER

The United Kingdom has a variable climate, which means that the weather changes rapidly from day to day. At the same time it is an equable climate, which means that usually there are no long periods of very hot or very cold, or very wet, or very dry weather. However, these average conditions conceal great differences between the different parts of the U.K. The north and west tend to be warmer and wetter in the winter than the south and east. However, in the summer the south and east tend to be hotter, drier, and sunnier than the north and west.

Weather can cause problems, especially during periods of fog, which may delay people traveling by road or air. Many highway pileups occur during fog, and despite having automatic landing systems, many planes are diverted to other airports because of foggy conditions.

Sometimes fog becomes smog. This happens when smoke, dirt, and other pollutants in the air become mixed with fog. Then air quality is very poor and can even cause breathing problems for some people.

Frost may cause difficulties, particularly if it comes toward the end of spring when it can kill the blossoms on fruit trees. Drivers, too, may be caught unawares by the frosty, slippery roads if the weather had previously been warm and springlike.

Drought has been a problem in recent years, especially 1976, 1984, 1989, 1990, and 1991. Long periods with little or no rainfall cause reservoir levels to fall. The use of hoses is banned, and people are urged to save and reuse water.

▼ *In January, eastern areas are colder than the west. In July, the south is warmer than Scotland and the north.*

▼ *The heaviest rain falls in the north and west of the U.K., especially Wales, the Lake District, the Pennines, and Scotland.*

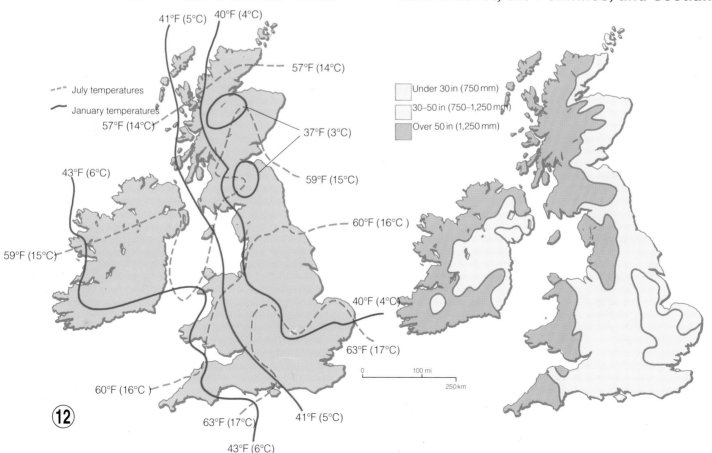

- - - July temperatures
—— January temperatures

Under 30 in (750 mm)
30–50 in (750–1,250 mm)
Over 50 in (1,250 mm)

41°F (5°C) 40°F (4°C)
57°F (14°C)
57°F (14°C)
37°F (3°C)
43°F (6°C)
59°F (15°C)
59°F (15°C)
60°F (16°C)
40°F (4°C)
63°F (17°C)
60°F (16°C)
63°F (17°C) 41°F (5°C)
43°F (6°C)

0   100 mi
250 km

Sometimes very high winds cause severe damage to homes and property. This damage was caused by the great gale across southern England in October 1987.

▶ Hot, sunny summers are good for business at British resorts like Ventnor on the Isle of Wight.

▼London, January 1991, and a traditional form of transportation comes to the rescue of a modern one!

KEY FACTS

● Since climatic records were first kept in the U.K. in the 1850s, the air temperature has risen by 0.9°F (0.5°C).
● The four warmest years on record were 1987, 1988, 1990, and 1991.
● If air temperatures continue to rise, the polar ice caps will melt, and sea levels will rise by 5 feet (1.5 m) by 2020, flooding much of southeast England and East Anglia.
● For every 1°F (0.6°C) rise in air temperature the death rate falls by 1.4% because people eat less food and suffer fewer heart attacks.

⊞ NATURAL RESOURCES

The United Kingdom is still rich in natural resources despite the rapid growth of industry in the last 250 years. Coal was the basis of the 19th-century British Industrial Revolution. Large industrial cities soon grew up on coalfields in South Wales, the Midlands, Lancashire, Yorkshire, Scotland, and northeast England. Despite such a long history of mining, the U.K. still has enough coal for the next 200 years. However this coal will be expensive to mine and contains high levels of sulfur. When this coal is burned it produces sulfur dioxide — one of the main causes of acid rain. In the future coal mined in the U.K. will have to compete with cheap coal imported from Poland, China, South Africa, and the U.S.

Oil and natural gas were discovered under the North Sea in the 1960s. Since then, they have become very important sources of power. Recently new power stations have been built to burn natural gas rather than coal. However no one knows how long the North Sea deposits of oil and gas will last. So the search for new deposits continues in the North Channel of the Irish Sea, between Scotland and Northern Ireland.

Nuclear power has proved to be a very expensive form of energy. Surprisingly, the main costs are not in building nuclear power stations but from the difficulty and danger of dismantling a nuclear power station at the end of its life. In fact, electricity generated by nuclear power stations is almost twice as expensive as electricity from coal-burning

KEY FACTS

● Oil provides 43% of the U.K.'s energy, coal 33%, natural gas 18%, nuclear power 5%, and hydroelectricity and other minor sources 1%.
● In 1979 the U.K. produced 134.6 million tons of coal. In 1991 the figure had dropped to 98.7 million tons.
● In 1979, 187,000 miners worked in British pits. In 1991 there were 58,000.
● More than 22 million tons of organic waste are thrown away each year. This could be used to produce methane gas for chemical synthesis.

◀ *The nuclear power station in Sizewell, Suffolk, is one of the Pressurized Water Reactors, or PWRs for short.*

This North Sea oil rig, with its support vessel nearby, is extracting oil and natural gas — vital British natural resources. There are more than 30 oil and gas rigs in the British portion of the North Sea.

power stations and three times as expensive as electricity from natural gas-burning power stations. Because of this, it seems very unlikely that new nuclear power stations will be built in the U.K.

Hydroelectricity is power generated by running water. It is important in remote parts of Scotland and Wales but is too expensive to transmit to the Midlands and southeast England where most people live. The estuaries of the Severn and Mersey rivers could be used to generate power from the rise and fall of the tides. However, these projects would be very expensive and could harm sensitive environments, such as wetlands.

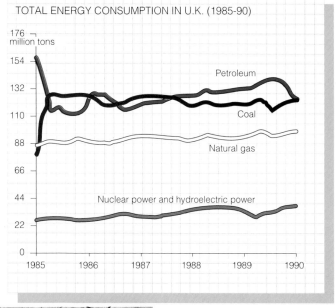

TOTAL ENERGY CONSUMPTION IN U.K. (1985-90)

176 million tons

154

132

110

88

66

44

22

0

1985   1986   1987   1988   1989   1990

Petroleum

Coal

Natural gas

Nuclear power and hydroelectric power

◄ Although the British coal industry is highly mechanized to help it compete with imports of cheaper foreign coal, the miners are as essential as ever.

In 1801, at the time of the first census, the United Kingdom was a country in which most people lived in the countryside and worked on farms. There were a few large towns like Bristol and Edinburgh, but London was the only big city. Factories in 1801 were small and used little machinery, and industries, such as weaving, were carried out in people's homes.

Things had changed greatly by the census of 1901. The Industrial Revolution transformed factories by using steam-powered machinery to do the work that had previously been done by hand. Big new factories, with big new machines, appeared on the coalfields of Scotland, northern England, and the Midlands. Cities like Manchester, Birmingham, Glasgow, and Belfast grew rapidly as people flocked from the countryside to find work in the new factories. London continued to grow as a

major port and industrial center, but the main area of population growth was in the Midlands and the north.

Since 1901, many heavy industries, such as coal mining, steel making, and shipbuilding, have declined. Many new industries, like electronics, have grown in southeast England. Here they are closer to their markets in Europe and to the Channel Tunnel. Between 1951 and 1991, many

◀ **Commuters stream across London Bridge on their way to work. Many have traveled a long way from their homes in the countryside.**

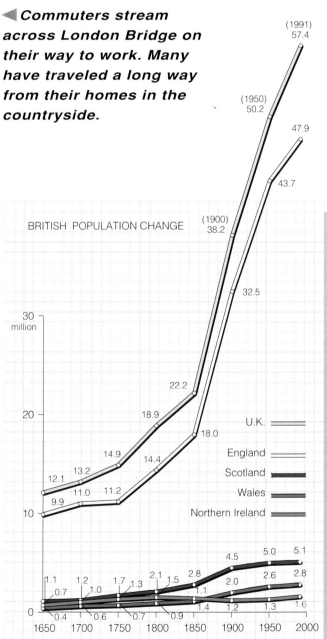

BRITISH POPULATION CHANGE

U.K.
England
Scotland
Wales
Northern Ireland

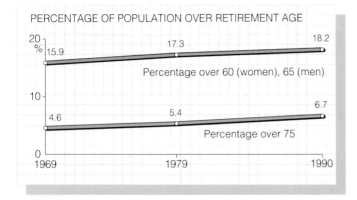

PERCENTAGE OF POPULATION OVER RETIREMENT AGE

Percentage over 60 (women), 65 (men)

15.9 — 17.3 — 18.2

Percentage over 75

4.6 — 5.4 — 6.7

1969 — 1979 — 1990

people moved from the northern parts of the U.K., where the number of new jobs was decreasing. They went to find work in the south and east, particularly in and around London.

Even in southeast England not all areas have increased their population. Slums and areas of poor housing in inner cities have been redeveloped. In the process, people have moved away from city centers toward the edges of the built-up areas, where new housing developments have been concentrated.

SENIOR CITIZENS

Britain is a country with high medical standards, where most people have a balanced diet. One result of this is that more people are living longer. This increase in the numbers of older people has important implications for services like health and housing. In the future the U.K. will need more retirement homes, nursing homes, and sheltered housing projects to care for the growing number of senior citizens. Similarly there may be a demand for more doctors, nurses, and hospitals specializing in the care of older people.

▼*Older people often move to places like Eastbourne because the mild seaside climate is beneficial to their health.*

When people reach the age of retirement many decide to move back to their hometown. More than two million people over 60 years old live at the seashore, in places like Southport, Eastbourne, Brighton, and Bournemouth. They are attracted by the scenery, the weather, and perhaps memories of holidays they spent in these places. The movement of retired people into these towns has led to a population increase in some of the main coastal areas of south and southwest England.

CITY VERSUS COUNTRY

Other groups of people are also on the move. In 1990 more than 20 percent of all COMMUTERS traveled more than 25 miles (40 km) to and from work every day. Despite the traffic jams and the extra time and travel costs, they believe that the benefits of living in the country are worth it, because they have experienced living in cities. Of the 20

▲ *Providing services in rural areas is a problem because of long distances between places. Mobile stores are one solution.*

percent of long-distance commuters, 17 percent used to live in cities and made deliberate decisions to move out.

In contrast, many city areas are more pleasant to live in than they were even 50 years ago. The decline of heavy industries, the change from coal-burning steam engines on the railroads to diesel engines, and the passing of legislation to control the POLLUTION of the atmosphere has improved some inner-city areas enormously.

ETHNIC GROUPS

The population of cities in the U.K. is made up of a large number of communities. All the people in these communities share the same basic needs: jobs, decent housing, and a secure environment in which to live.

KEY FACTS

● The population of England and Wales grew by 0.5% between 1981 and 1991; in Northern Ireland it grew by 0.1%, but in Scotland it fell by 0.1% between the same years.

● The Central Mosque in London has a congregation of 60,000, making it one of the largest mosques in a non-Muslim country.

● Ten percent of the population of the U.K. move home each year.

● Forty percent of the U.K.'s Afro-Caribbean and Asian population was born in the U.K.

● The average life expectancy for women is 75 years, and for men it is 71 years.

In the 1950s and 1960s people from the West Indies, India, Pakistan, and Bangladesh were encouraged to come live and work in the U.K. There was a labor shortage, and the U.K. needed all the workers it could get. Many of these people went to cities like London and Birmingham where there were jobs. However, the newcomers often had to live in run-down parts of the cities, and many faced prejudice at work and in the community. By 1992, the U.K.'s 2.4 million Afro-Caribbean and Asian population made up 4 percent of its total population.

▼ *Street markets still thrive in some towns and cities, particularly in poorer areas. Stands are cheaper to run than stores, so market prices are lower.*

EDUCATION

All children must start school at 5 years of age and continue until they are 16. There are two systems of education. One is free and maintained by government funds. The other is private education where parents pay the tuition. Confusingly, these schools are often called public schools. Up to the age of 5, children can attend nursery schools and kindergartens, if these are available in their area. From the ages of 5 to 11, children attend primary schools, although a few may go to middle schools when they are 9 and stay until 13. After they are 11, children go on to secondary schools, most of which are comprehensive, although there are also the selective public schools that charge a tuition.

Children take GCSE (General Certificate of Secondary Education) examinations at age 16, and some go on to take A levels or other exams at 18 or 19. Some students continue on to universities or colleges. In Scotland there are no GCSE or A level exams. Instead, the exams are known as Highers.

LEISURE ACTIVITIES

People in the U.K. now enjoy more leisure time, and as a result, membership in sports clubs has increased by 60 percent in the last ten years. Some people prefer to spend their leisure time watching soccer or cricket matches, while others prefer more active pursuits, such as cycling, climbing, skiing, and windsurfing. Fishing is still the most popular participation sport. Leisure activities new to the U.K., such as American football and baseball, are becoming popular.

Pressure on COUNTRY PARKS close to large towns is increasing, especially during weekends and holidays when thousands of visitors may flock to them to enjoy the

◀ *The U.K. has both state (above) and independent (left) schools. The funds to run state schools come from the taxes everyone pays. Independent schools get their money by charging tuition. Both types of schools try to provide a broad, balanced curriculum.*

KEY FACTS

● In 1991, 98% of all households in the U.K. had a television, 55% had a video recorder, and 20% a home computer.

● In 1991, 4,241,000 children attended state primary schools, and 3,551,000 attended state secondary schools. There were 641,000 children in independent primary and secondary (public) schools.

● The *Sun* is the best-selling British newspaper. It is read by 10.8 million people every day. Second is the *Daily Mirror* with 8.8 million readers.

● In contrast only 1.1 million people read *The Times* every day, and 0.7 million read the *Financial Times*.

▼ *Regional celebrations are an important way to keep local traditions alive. Here, in Luss, Scotland, children take part in a Highland dancing competition, as their families have done for generations.*

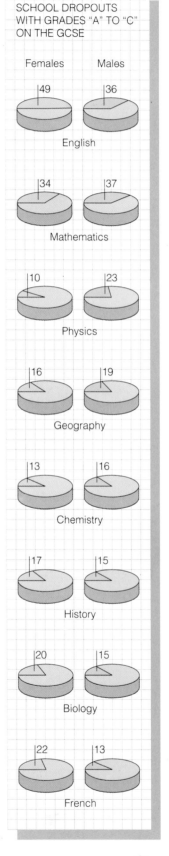

SCHOOL DROPOUTS WITH GRADES "A" TO "C" ON THE GCSE

Females	Males
49	36

English

| 34 | 37 |

Mathematics

| 10 | 23 |

Physics

| 16 | 19 |

Geography

| 13 | 16 |

Chemistry

| 17 | 15 |

History

| 20 | 15 |

Biology

| 22 | 13 |

French

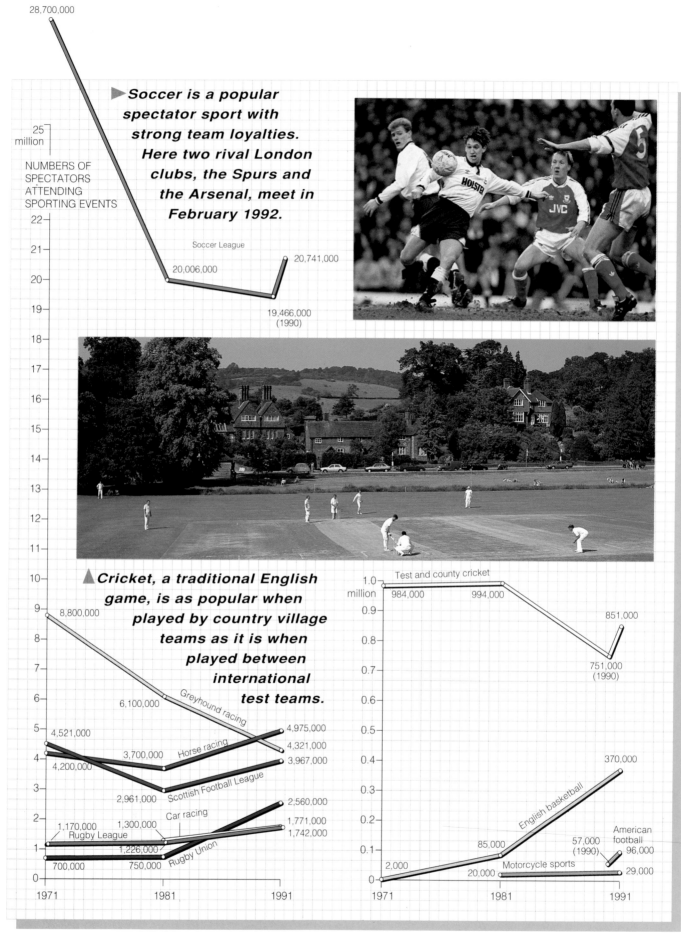

28,700,000

25 million

NUMBERS OF SPECTATORS ATTENDING SPORTING EVENTS

22
21
20
19
18
17
16
15
14
13
12
11
10
9
8
7
6
5
4
3
2
1
0

►*Soccer is a popular spectator sport with strong team loyalties. Here two rival London clubs, the Spurs and the Arsenal, meet in February 1992.*

Soccer League

20,006,000

20,741,000

19,466,000 (1990)

▲*Cricket, a traditional English game, is as popular when played by country village teams as it is when played between international test teams.*

8,800,000

4,521,000

4,200,000

Greyhound racing

6,100,000

Horse racing

3,700,000

4,975,000

4,321,000

3,967,000

Scottish Football League

2,961,000

Car racing

2,560,000

1,170,000

1,300,000

1,771,000

1,742,000

Rugby League

1,226,000

Rugby Union

700,000

750,000

1971   1981   1991

1.0 million

Test and county cricket

984,000   994,000

851,000

0.9

0.8

0.7

0.6

0.5

0.4

0.3

0.2

0.1

0

751,000 (1990)

370,000

English basketball

85,000

57,000 (1990)

American football

96,000

2,000

20,000

Motorcycle sports

29,000

1971   1981   1991

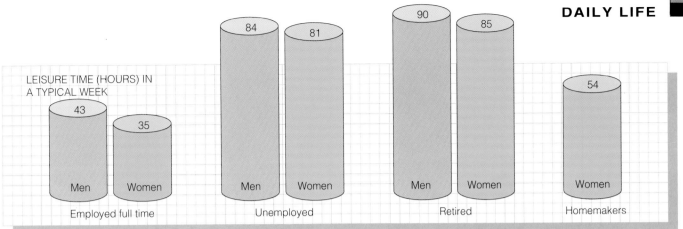

LEISURE TIME (HOURS) IN A TYPICAL WEEK

Employed full time		Unemployed		Retired		Homemakers
Men	Women	Men	Women	Men	Women	Women
43	35	84	81	90	85	54

scenery. At the same time more and more people are visiting NATIONAL PARKS. For example, each year 14 million people visit the Lake District, and 8 million visit the Yorkshire Dales national parks. This can cause over-crowding and congestion and damage the very environment people have come to enjoy.

THE MEDIA

Newspapers, magazines, and books are important sources of information and entertainment in the U.K. People in the U.K. read more newspapers than anywhere in the world, except the U.S. and Canada. There are more than 120 daily and Sunday newspapers, and no paper is directly owned by a political party. Recently the number of magazines sold has increased. This is partly because people have more leisure time and partly because there is a growing interest in leisure activities, such as gardening, cooking, photography, and DIY (Do-It-Yourself) home improvement.

Radio listeners and television viewers have an increasing number of channels from which to choose. The British Broadcasting Corporation runs two television channels (BBC 1 and BBC 2), together with five national radio channels and many local radio stations. There are 14 independent TV channels.

▶ *The sales of regional newspapers, like this one in northeast England, have grown by 2% over the last five years. People still like to buy local papers to catch up with local issues.*

Each year, the queen, as sovereign and head of state, opens Parliament to symbolize the link between Crown and government.

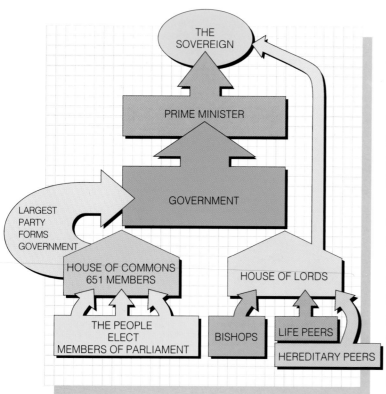

Great Bitain's type of government is called a constitutional monarchy. This means that the sovereign (currently Queen Elizabeth II) is head of state but that political power is in the hands of Parliament. There are two Houses of Parliament. The House of Commons has 651 members who are elected by the voters for a maximum of five years. The House of Lords is made up of hereditary peers (whose titles are handed down from parent to child) and life peers (whose titles are given only for the peer's lifetime). The government is formed within the House of Commons from the political party that has a majority over all the other parties. The leader of this political party becomes prime minister who, in turn, appoints a cabinet to supervise the day-to-day running of the country.

The main British political groups are the Conservative, Labor, and Liberal Democrat parties. There are also Scottish and Welsh Nationalist parties, along with the Democratic Unionist, Ulster Unionist, Social Democratic and Labor, and Sinn Fein parties in Northern Ireland.

In England, Wales, and Scotland there are three levels of local government: county or metropolitan councils, district councils, and parish councils. Northern Ireland has one level of 26 district councils.

The utilities and services that are needed are provided by different groups or organizations. Water and electricity, for example, are provided by specialist companies. Some services are provided by local branches of the central government, such as the Department of Social Security, which deals with pensions and other benefits. Other services, such as education, are provided by local government. In some parts of the country garbage collection and street cleaning are also provided by local government, but in other parts private companies do the work for government.

▼ *There are strict laws in the U.K. about drinking and driving. At the scene of an accident the police use a Breathalyzer® to check if the driver has too much alcohol in his bloodstream. There are now more than 1,000 more police officers in the U.K. than in 1983, and deaths from drunk driving have fallen by 10% in the same period.*

KEY FACTS

● Car crimes increased by more than 50% between 1990 and 1991.
● The number of burglaries reported to the police increased by 20% between 1990 and 1991.
● In 1981, 44,500 men were in British jails. In 1990 there were 48,500 men in jail.
● In 1981 there were 1,400 women in prison in the U.K. In 1990 there were 1,800 women in prison.

⚒ FOOD AND FARMING

arming in the U.K. has changed a great deal in the last 30 years. In general, farms have become larger, using more machines and chemicals but employing fewer workers. Some people now refer to British farming as AGRIBUSINESS — an intensive form of agriculture that uses chemicals and machines to produce the maximum output of crops and animals at the lowest cost, which, in turn, means cheaper food for consumers.

These changes in farming have had important effects on the countryside. Big machines, such as combine harvesters, need big fields in which to operate, so rows of trees and bushes have been removed to create the larger fields. The trees and bushes used to provide an important HABITAT for wildlife. Their numbers have fallen drastically as their habitat has been removed. Nitrogen from artificial fertilizers has found its way into supplies of drinking water where it causes serious pollution. Many insects, reptiles, and birds have been killed by chemical pesticide sprays.

Loss of habitat is not only caused by removing trees and bushes. Wetlands are being drained endangering the common frogs, newts, and toads in some places. As people move into the country, many convert old farm buildings into homes. These buildings were important nesting and roosting places for barn owls, which are now also endangered.

Larger fields are more at risk from soil erosion — the removal of the topsoil by wind or water. In areas like East Anglia great clouds of soil have been blown away from the huge fields.

▼ *In areas of the U.K., such as Wales, where the soil is too poor for cattle and crops, sheep farming is very important.*

KEY FACTS

● More than 8% of the population of the U.K. is now vegetarian, and the number is increasing every year.

● In 1991 people spent $859 million on fish and chips, $441 million on hamburger meals, and $395 million on chicken meals.

● In 1965 there were 210,000 farm workers in the U.K. In 1991 the number had dropped to 102,000.

● Between 1945 and 1990, the U.K. lost 60% of its wide open land, 90% of its natural ponds, 25% of its rows of trees and bushes, and 80% of its ancient woodlands.

However, farming is changing yet again. Some farmers have taken up ORGANIC FARMING using traditional fertilizers, such as manure, and are replanting rows of trees and bushes. As shoppers demand more organically grown fruit, vegetables, and meat, pressure on farmland has been reduced.

Farmers in Britain are deeply affected by the Common Agricultural Policy (CAP) of the European Community (EC). The aim of the policy is to give farmers throughout the EC a fair standard of living and to ensure that there is a reliable supply of food for everyone at reasonable prices. The policy works by setting a guaranteed minimum price for farm produce. This means farmers know they will be able to sell their goods and make a profit.

In the 1980s the EC wanted to encourage farmers to grow more cereals, such as

▲ *Rapeseed oil is a popular crop because the EC pays a lot for it.*

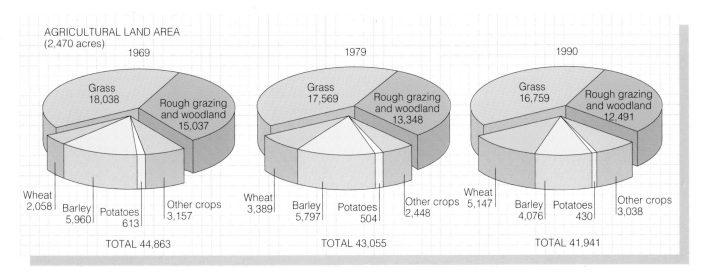

AGRICULTURAL LAND AREA
(2,470 acres)

1969

Grass 18,038
Rough grazing and woodland 15,037
Wheat 2,058
Barley 5,960
Potatoes 613
Other crops 3,157

TOTAL 44,863

1979

Grass 17,569
Rough grazing and woodland 13,348
Wheat 3,389
Barley 5,797
Potatoes 504
Other crops 2,448

TOTAL 43,055

1990

Grass 16,759
Rough grazing and woodland 12,491
Wheat 5,147
Barley 4,076
Potatoes 430
Other crops 3,038

TOTAL 41,941

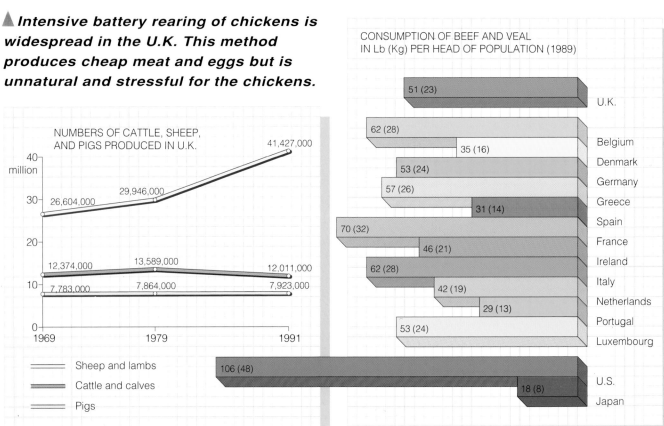

▲ *Intensive battery rearing of chickens is widespread in the U.K. This method produces cheap meat and eggs but is unnatural and stressful for the chickens.*

NUMBERS OF CATTLE, SHEEP, AND PIGS PRODUCED IN U.K.

41,427,000

40 million

29,946,000

30   26,604,000

20

12,374,000   13,589,000   12,011,000

10   7,783,000   7,864,000   7,923,000

0
1969   1979   1991

— Sheep and lambs
— Cattle and calves
— Pigs

CONSUMPTION OF BEEF AND VEAL IN Lb (Kg) PER HEAD OF POPULATION (1989)

51 (23)		U.K.
62 (28)		Belgium
	35 (16)	Denmark
53 (24)		Germany
57 (26)		Greece
	31 (14)	Spain
70 (32)		France
	46 (21)	Ireland
62 (28)		Italy
	42 (19)	Netherlands
	29 (13)	Portugal
53 (24)		Luxembourg
106 (48)		U.S.
	18 (8)	Japan

wheat and corn, so high prices were set for these crops. If farmers produced more than the EC needed, the surplus was stored in warehouses. The same thing happened with beef, milk, and wine. In order to reduce the surpluses, the EC sometimes gives away products, like butter, cheese, and beef, to senior citizens and other needy groups. However, the EC is now trying to cut down the surpluses by establishing an agreed maximum amount, or QUOTA, for the milk, beef, lamb, and other products that each farm can produce. Another method of reducing surpluses is to lower the guaranteed price for crops like wheat and barley. These changes in EC policy mean that British farmers, the most efficient in the EC, have had to adapt the crops they grow or the animals that they raise in order to stay in business.

The growth of country-wide supermarket chains, as well as improved transportation and refrigeration, has helped reduce the variety of regional foods. But the names of well-known foods and dishes give a hint of that variety: Cornish pasties, Lancashire hot-pot, Yorkshire pudding, haggis, Arbroath smokies, Welsh cakes, Bath buns, are just a few. Then, of course, there are cheeses. Stilton, Cheshire, and Cheddar are known all around the world, but to get away from the dull, uniform varieties that once were all the supermarkets stocked, smaller cheese makers have revived older, local varieties: Blue Vinney from Dorset, Cashel Blue from Ireland, the small round cheeses of Orkney, and many more.

▼ *In remote parts of Scotland, farms, like this field on the Isle of Skye, are abandoned as people move to towns.*

⦿ TRADE AND INDUSTRY

During the 19th century, British industries, such as coal, steel, ship-building, and engineering, grew very rapidly. New mines, factories, roads, railroads, and ports were built. Great Britain became the world's first industrial nation, exporting its goods all over the world. Areas like south Wales, the Midlands, Merseyside, Manchester, west Yorkshire, central Scotland, London, and Newcastle became important industrial centers. The basis of all this growth was the manufacturing industry — industries that change raw materials like iron or wool into finished products.

However, in the last 15 years these manufacturing industries have begun to decline. Factories have closed, and people have lost their jobs. Some industries such as steel, shipbuilding, coal-mining, and engineering have been particularly hard hit. Many industries such as car manufacturing have declined because of fierce competition from foreign companies. The textile industry has also suffered because of competition from cheap imported goods. Other reasons for the decline of the manufacturing industry include poor management, a failure to introduce new technology, a lack of investment, and a lack of government support. This decline has hit the 19th-century industrial areas, such as

▼ **Old industrial areas, like the Albert Dock in Liverpool, are being redeveloped to revive the local economy and provide new jobs.**

◀ *Some of the most exciting modern architecture has been commissioned by industrial companies. This company headquarters and factory in Bristol is very different from the 19th-century industrial buildings (opposite).*

south Wales, the Midlands, and central Scotland, particularly hard. Empty, abandoned factories and high rates of unemployment have created urban and social problems.

However, some new industries, like microelectronics, have developed to replace the old ones. Britain is developing its high-technology (HIGH-TECH) industries involved in making computers, electronics, and telecommunications equipment. Most of these new GROWTH INDUSTRIES are located in a belt between London and Bristol, with smaller clusters in East Anglia and Scotland.

THE CAR INDUSTRY

The British car industry has faced a great deal of competition from foreign imports since the 1970s. Foreign cars were cheaper and in some cases more reliable. The main problem was that in 1978 each Japanese car worker produced 30 cars per year, while the British car worker only produced seven.

During the 1980s, British car manufacturers

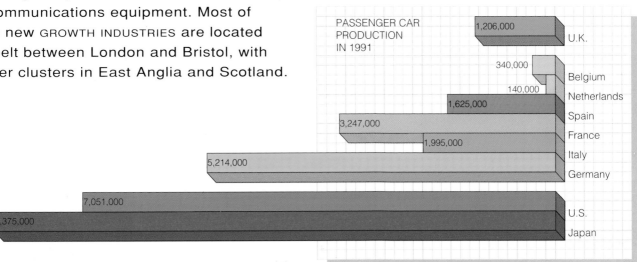

PASSENGER CAR PRODUCTION IN 1991

	Production
U.K.	1,206,000
Belgium	340,000
Netherlands	140,000
Spain	1,625,000
France	3,247,000
Italy	1,995,000
Germany	5,214,000
U.S.	7,051,000
Japan	8,375,000

◀ **Tourism is now a major industry in the U.K., attracting visitors from all over the world. Two of the most popular attractions are Stratford-upon-** **Avon (left) with its associations with Shakespeare, and Windsor Castle (above) and the guards in their traditional uniforms.**

fought back. They introduced new products and new technology, such as automatic welding robots on the assembly line. However, some British car makers were taken over by foreign companies. Hillman was taken over by Peugeot, and General Motors took over Vauxhall. More and more car production is dominated by MULTINATIONAL companies — companies with their head-quarters in one country and factories in many others. Now many British car workers are employed by foreign-run companies, such as Ford (U.S.), Peugeot/Talbot

SHIPBUILDING (1990)
(Tons)

Country	Tons
U.K.	186,400
Belgium	69,000
Denmark	161,200
Germany	642,700
Greece	42,700
Spain	421,700
France	94,800
Italy	562,400
Netherlands	97,000
Portugal	71,200
U.S.	29,300
Japan	3,251,100

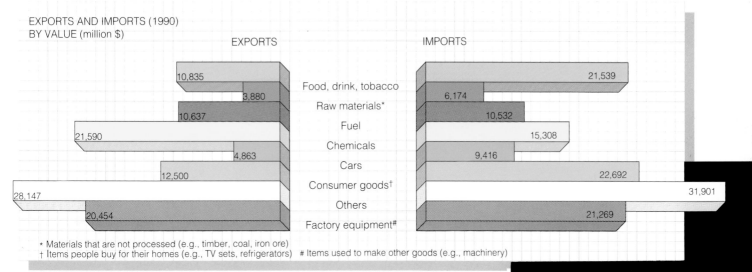

EXPORTS AND IMPORTS (1990)
BY VALUE (million $)

	EXPORTS		IMPORTS
Food, drink, tobacco	10,835		21,539
Raw materials*	3,880		6,174
Fuel	10,637		10,532
Chemicals	21,590		15,308
Cars	4,863		9,416
Consumer goods†	12,500		22,692
Others	28,147		31,901
Factory equipment#	20,454		21,269

* Materials that are not processed (e.g., timber, coal, iron ore)
† Items people buy for their homes (e.g., TV sets, refrigerators) # Items used to make other goods (e.g., machinery)

(France), Fiat (Italy,) and Nissan and Toyota (Japan).

The Nissan car factory in Washington New Town near Sunderland is an example of a factory built by a multinational company. Nissan wanted a base within the European Community from which to make cars for sale throughout Europe. The company was attracted to Sunderland by

▼ *In the Stock Exchange's currency trading room dealers buy and sell the world's main currencies from dollars to yen.*

KEY FACTS

● In 1913 the U.K. built 59% of all the world's ships. By 1991, the figure was down to 2%.
● In Japan the government pays 38% of the cost of each ship built. In South Korea the figure is 40%, but in the U.K. it is 21%.
● In 1972, 76% of the 1.2 million new cars sold in the U.K. were made there. By 1990, only 37% of the 1.9 million new cars were made in the U.K.
● The U.K.'s pop music industry is a major "export", worth more than $758 million each year.
● The financial services sector, which includes banking, insurance, and the Stock Exchange, earned more than $3.8 billion in exports in 1991.

government grants and other financial help. An important aspect of these multinational companies is that they are controlled from outside the U.K. This means that decisions about factory closures or layoffs may be made thousands of miles away. However, foreign-owned car companies are important sources of jobs, and their expansion has provided work for more than 10,000 people since 1989. By 1991, workers in Japanese-run car factories in the U.K. were producing 20 cars a year, and the figure is still rising.

SERVICE INDUSTRIES
Although the manufacturing industry has declined in the U.K. in the last ten years, SERVICE INDUSTRIES, such as banking and

insurance, have grown. There are three main groups that make up these service industries: transportation, finance (including insurance, banking, and property), and education, health, and recreation. Service industries have become important because they affect people in all aspects of their lives. Every time we visit a store, make a telephone call, go to school, turn on water, gas, or electricity, or visit a bank or social security office we are using a service industry. Service industries, as the term suggests, provide services that people need.

Jobs in service industries are not spread evenly across the U.K. Between 1979 and 1990, service industries grew by 7 percent, which translates into 870,000 jobs. However,

90 percent of these jobs were in only four areas: southeast England, East Anglia, the southwest, and the Midlands. One of the fastest growing service industries has been business services, including advertising, market research, security, and catering. Between 1985 and 1990, 215,000 new jobs were created in this group of service industries alone. The hotel and catering group of service industries created another 120,000 new jobs between 1985 and 1990. The main groups of people who benefited from the growth of service industries were women, part-time workers, and young people. As a result, all these new jobs were of little help to the people who had been unemployed for a long time. Recently the expansion of service industries has slowed, but they have now become one of the most important sectors of industry in the U.K.

ENCOURAGING INDUSTRIES AND EMPLOYMENT

In areas where unemployment is high the government is eager to encourage the growth of new industries that will provide more jobs. Areas with high unemployment may have other problems, such as many abandoned factories and large areas of wasteland. In some of these places the local councils have established special ENTERPRISE ZONES to encourage firms to come to the area and create jobs.

To encourage companies to come to the enterprise zones, the councils offer low rents and ten years in which the companies do not have to pay business rates. Planning procedures for new factories and office developments in the enterprise zones are also made simpler and quicker, so it is easier for companies to get permission to set up their businesses. In this way, enterprise zones from Clydebank in Scotland to Dudley in the West Midlands to London's Dockland have developed and grown.

Some cities, like Liverpool, have set up urban development corporations to redevelop run-down parts of the city to attract new industries. Urban development corporations are larger than enterprise zones and work by improving the local environment. For example, the development corporations demolish abandoned factories and build new roads and new factories. They cannot offer freedom from business rates, but they are able to obtain money from the government and private companies to improve the area and build new modern factories.

◀ At Felixstowe docks, Suffolk, a ship is loaded with cargo containers. These are an efficient way of transporting imports and exports.

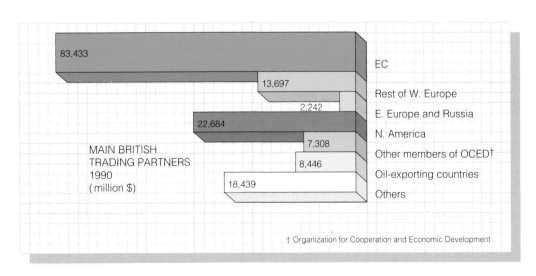

MAIN BRITISH TRADING PARTNERS 1990 (million $)

83,433	EC
13,697	Rest of W. Europe
2,242	E. Europe and Russia
22,684	N. America
7,308	Other members of OCED†
8,446	Oil-exporting countries
18,439	Others

† Organization for Cooperation and Economic Development

✦ TRANSPORTATION

An efficient transportation system is vital for moving people and goods around the U.K. Road transportation has increased in importance during the last ten years, for both people and goods. More than 95 percent of all goods moved in the U.K. now travel by road, and by 1991, there were over 400,000 more cars on British roads than in 1985. However, this expansion of road transportation has created severe traffic jams in towns. Increased traffic means accidents are becoming more frequent, and air pollution from vehicle exhausts has increased. New highways have been built at the expense of areas of valuable countryside, and noise pollution has become more widespread. Attempts to solve these problems by introducing park-and-ride programs, bus lanes, or tidal flow plans have been limited.

▲ *Commuters using the M4 highway face traffic jams like this every morning and evening as they travel to and from London.*

British Rail has suffered from rising fuel costs, an aging system of tracks that is expensive to maintain, competition from road haulage, low investment, and pressures from commuters in southeast England. To meet these challenges, British Rail has introduced computer signaling, and specialized traffic, such as flatcars, which take containers of internationally agreed standard sizes. Newer and faster train services have been introduced, and the Channel Tunnel is giving a boost to rail services, especially in the southeast.

Air transportation continues to grow in importance, especially for passengers.

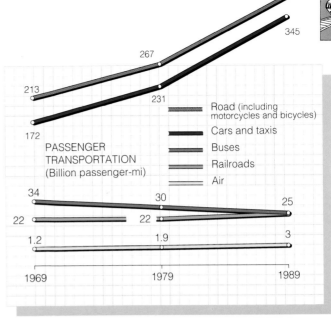

There are regular services between London and major U.K. cities, such as Glasgow and Belfast. London (Heathrow, Stanstead, and Gatwick) plus Manchester, Glasgow, and Birmingham have important international services. Apart from passengers, airlines carry perishable goods, such as flowers, and light, valuable goods, such as watches or jewelry.

Little freight travels on the U.K.'s rivers and canals. Nevertheless, the canals are becoming increasingly important centers of tourism.

Because the U.K. is an island, freight transportation by sea is important. The use of containers in which goods are packed at factories has speeded up the loading and unloading of cargo at ports, such as Tilbury, Harwich, Felixstowe, and Southampton. The Channel Tunnel may reduce the number of passengers using cross-channel ferries and ports, such as Dover, which had 7.2 million passengers in 1991, but the ferries are likely to remain important for the forseeable future.

PASSENGER TRANSPORTATION (Billion passenger-mi)

- Road (including motorcycles and bicycles)
- Cars and taxis
- Buses
- Railroads
- Air

	1969	1979	1989
	213	267	378
	172	231	345
	34	30	25
	22	22	25
	1.2	1.9	3

KEY FACTS

● Twenty-two percent of all the energy used in the U.K. each year is consumed by transportation.

● About 99% of the energy used by British transportation is in the form of oil.

● In 1970, 34% of the people traveled to work by bus. By 1991, the figure was only 25%.

● In 1970, 43% of the people traveled to work by car. By 1991, the figure was 62%.

◀ *New types of transportation, such as the Docklands Light Railway (left) and the new Manchester "tramway" system, help to get people to and from work quickly without polluting the environment.*

🏴󠁧󠁢󠁥󠁮󠁧󠁿 THE ENVIRONMENT

There is serious concern in the U.K. about the quality of the environment. People agree on the need to ensure that the environment is improved to achieve a better future for the nation's children, but they disagree about the best way to do it. Some people argue that the pollution of the U.K.'s rivers and oceans is so serious that immediate action is needed. Factories still pollute rivers and oceans with toxic chemicals, while untreated sewage from towns and cities is still pumped into the ocean. Oil tankers sometimes pollute seas and rivers by discharging oil into the water. There are regulations to prevent these types of pollution, but they are difficult to enforce. Other people are in favor of trying to persuade polluters not to make things worse rather than fining them for doing so.

Air quality varies from place to place in the U.K. In general the air quality in towns and cities is poor because of fumes from factories and from car exhausts. There are measures to reduce pollution by fitting catalytic converters to car exhausts and trying to persuade more people to use public transportation. So far improvements have been slow.

Acid rain is a problem that also affects many European countries besides the U.K.

▼ *The photo shows why Lochain na h'Achlaise and the Black Mount in Perthshire are protected as areas of outstanding natural beauty.*

EMISSIONS OF
SULFUR DIOXIDE (SO$_2$)
PER PERSON (1990)
(tons)

U.K.	70
Belgium	94
Denmark	76
Germany	64
Greece	62
Spain	72
France	35
Ireland	43
Italy	44
Luxembourg	40
Netherlands	19
Portugal	30
U.S.	100
Japan	12

►*Factory waste being discharged into the ocean at Humberside. In the background is a chemical factory.*

▲ *People in the U.K. care about the environment and will protest against developments they dislike. The protest here is against the Channel Tunnel.*

Norway and Sweden receive the sulfur dioxide that forms acid rain from power stations in the U.K. The westerly winds blow the pollution from power stations in the U.K. and elsewhere in Europe across the continent. The acid rain kills trees and even fish in lakes in Wales and Scotland. Therefore there is great pressure on British power stations to burn fuels, like natural gas, which are low in sulfur. It is also possible to fit special equipment in power stations that burn sulfur-producing fuels, like coal, but the equipment is very expensive.

National parks, country parks, and areas of outstanding natural beauty have been set up to preserve areas of particularly beautiful countryside. The aim is to restrict development in these areas so that future generations will be able to enjoy them, even if land in other areas is polluted by factories, farms, or towns.

THE FUTURE

One way of thinking about the U.K. in the future is to consider how far present trends in industry, farming, leisure, and other areas are likely to continue. In the countryside people will probably continue to leave very remote areas, such as parts of Scotland and Wales, where it is hard to earn a living. Providing services, such as schools, hospitals, and libraries, is a problem in some rural areas, and this is likely to get worse.

Farming is already using less land, so the land that once grew crops may in the future be used for golf courses or riding stables. More people will have more leisure time in the future, so even more visitors will flock to areas of beautiful countryside, like national parks. Because so many different groups often want to use the same area of countryside, conflicts will arise. There are already disputes in some places between hikers and motorcyclists, and horseback riders and mountain bikers. In the future planners will need to manage areas of the countryside carefully in order to reduce these conflicts.

Sources of RENEWABLE ENERGY, which depend on wind, wave, or tidal power, may, in the future, replace some of the coal, oil, and natural gas used in the U.K. However, the search for new deposits of oil and gas will continue on both land and sea.

Water has been recognized as an

▼ *Princes Square, Glasgow, shows how shopping centers in the future may be enclosed, air-conditioned, and centrally heated.*

increasingly important resource. A recent series of dry years has emphasized the problem, particularly in the southern and eastern parts of the U.K., where the use of hoses to water gardens and wash cars has been banned. Scotland, Wales, and northwest England get the heaviest rain — often more than 39 inches (1,000 mm) a year.

However, the biggest demand for water for homes, factories and farms is in East Anglia and the southeast. There are ambitious plans to move large volumes of water from lakes and reservoirs in the west, along rivers like the Thames and Severn, to the south. This would be very complicated, and new canals would have to be dug to connect major rivers in order

KEY FACTS

● Geographers predict that growth and prosperity in the U.K. over the next 20 years will be concentrated in towns south of Oxford and east of Bristol. There will also be pockets of prosperity in other places, for example in Edinburgh and parts of Devon and Cornwall.
● Government spending to support declining regions will be highest in Scotland, Wales, and Northern Ireland. In 1990 the government spent $1,029 per person in Scotland, $1,094 in Wales, and $1,924 in Northern Ireland.
● Inner-city areas lost population at the rate of more than 8% between 1981 and 1991, a trend that is likely to continue.

▼ *The power of the future? Salter's Duck is a way of harnessing the energy produced by waves. So far it is only experimental.*

to get the water to the places that need it most.

New industries, perhaps based in the countryside and using local craftspeople to produce pottery, textiles, high fashion, or even electronic goods, are likely to develop strongly. At the other end of the scale, multinational companies seem ready to continue getting even larger as they take over or merge with other companies around the world. As a result even more office buildings will spring up in city centers, and more people will continue to leave towns and cities in search of a better QUALITY OF LIFE in the outer suburbs or in villages. From this it follows that the cost of travel in towns and cities is likely to keep rising. Sadly, pollution in both towns and in the countryside will remain a problem.

FURTHER INFORMATION

The following organizations are sources of information about the U.K. Most can provide up-to-date booklets, maps, and a host of statistics and other information.

BRITISH AIRPORTS AUTHORITY
2 Buckingham Gate, London SW1, England

BRITISH EMBASSY
3100 Massachusetts Avenue, NW, Washington, D.C. 20008

BRITISH TOURIST AUTHORITY
40 West 57th Street, New York, NY 10019

BRITRAIL TRAVEL INTERNATIONAL
1500 Broadway, New York, NY 10036

EC DELEGATION TO THE UNITED STATES
2100 M Street, NW, Suite 707, Washington, D.C. 20037

FRIENDS OF THE EARTH
218 D Street, SE, Washington, D.C. 20003

GREENPEACE
P.O. Box 96128, Washington, D.C. 20090

WORLD WILDLIFE FUND
1250 24th Street, NW, Washington, D.C. 20037

The following books may be useful for further project work:

Binney, Don. *Inside Great Britain.* Watts, 1988
Davies, Kath. *Wales.* Raintree Steck-Vaughn, 1990
Grant, Neil. *United Kingdom.* Silver Burdett, 1988
Peplow, Mary, and Shipley, Debra. *England.* Raintree Steck-Vaughn, 1990
Taylor, Doreen. *Scotland.* Raintree Steck-Vaughn, 1990

GLOSSARY

AGRIBUSINESS
Modern, intensive farming that uses chemicals and machines to increase production

COMMUTER
Person who travels some distance to and from work each day, from one area or district to another

COUNTRY PARK
Area of countryside planned and organized for recreation

ENTERPRISE ZONE
Particular areas in towns that receive special government help to create jobs and attract new industry

ENVIRONMENT
All the things that surround us such as people, buildings, and natural resources

FJORD
A valley formed by a glacier and then flooded because of a rise in the sea level

GROWTH INDUSTRIES
Industries that are expanding and becoming more important

HABITAT
A suitable place for particular types of wildlife and plants to live

HIGH-TECH
Industries that use the most up-to-date equipment, such as robots, to produce goods, such as computers

MULTINATIONAL
Large company with branches in many countries

NATIONAL PARKS
Large, mainly rural areas where the natural scenery and wildlife are protected for public enjoyment

ORGANIC FARMING
A system of agriculture that uses no artificial pesticides or fertilizers

POLLUTION
Harmful effect on the environment caused by human activity, e.g., noise, dirt

QUALITY OF LIFE
Level of well-being of a community and the area in which the community lives

QUOTA
Amount of goods allowed, e.g., the amount of milk that can be produced for sale by one farm

RENEWABLE ENERGY
Energy produced by a source that will not run out, e.g., wind, water

RIA
A river valley drowned by the sea due to a rise in the sea level

SEA-LOCH
A lake that has been drowned by a rise in the sea level

SERVICE INDUSTRY
Business that produces a service for the consumer, e.g., banking, health, transportation

INDEX

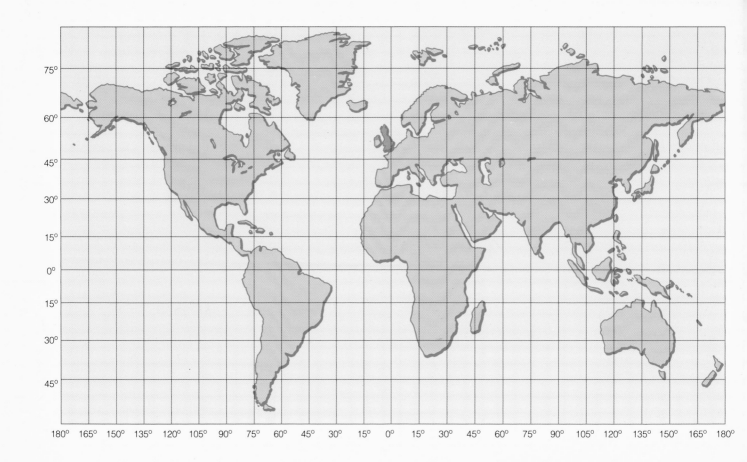

THE UNITED KINGDOM

ATLANTIC

OCEAN

ORKNEY
ISLANDS

SHETLAND
ISLANDS

OUTER HEBRIDES

INNER HEBRIDES

SCOTLAND

Aberdeen

NORTH

SEA

Glasgow

Edinburgh

55°

Londonderry

N. IRELAND

Newcastle upon Tyne

Belfast

Middlesbrough

IRISH
SEA

York

IRELAND

Preston

Leeds

Liverpool

Manchester

Nottingham

ENGLAND

Birmingham

WALES

LONDON

Swansea

Cardiff

Bristol

Southampton

Plymouth

ENGLISH CHANNEL

0°

FRANCE

0 — 100 mi

250 km